# Dear Parent:

Congratulations! Your child is taking the first steps on an exciting journey. The destination? Independent reading!

**STEP INTO READING®** will help your child get there. The program offers five steps to reading success. Each step includes fun stories and colorful art. There are also Step into Reading Sticker Books, Step into Reading Math Readers, Step into Reading Write-In Readers, Step into Reading Phonics Readers, and Step into Reading Phonics First Steps! Boxed Sets—a complete literacy program with something for every child.

## Learning to Read, Step by Step!

**Ready to Read** Preschool–Kindergarten
• big type and easy words • rhyme and rhythm • picture clues
For children who know the alphabet and are eager to begin reading.

**Reading with Help** Preschool–Grade 1
• basic vocabulary • short sentences • simple stories
For children who recognize familiar words and sound out new words with help.

**Reading on Your Own** Grades 1–3
• engaging characters • easy-to-follow plots • popular topics
For children who are ready to read on their own.

**Reading Paragraphs** Grades 2–3
• challenging vocabulary • short paragraphs • exciting stories
For newly independent readers who read simple sentences with confidence.

**Ready for Chapters** Grades 2–4
• chapters • longer paragraphs • full-color art
For children who want to take the plunge into chapter books but still like colorful pictures.

**STEP INTO READING®** is designed to give every child a successful reading experience. The grade levels are only guides. Children can progress through the steps at their own speed, developing confidence in their reading, no matter what their grade.

Remember, a lifetime love of reading starts with a single step!

BARBIE and associated trademarks and trade dress are owned by, and used under license from, Mattel, Inc. © 2006 Mattel, Inc. All Rights Reserved.
Published in the United States by Random House Children's Books, a division of Random House, Inc., New York, and simultaneously in Canada by Random House of Canada Limited, Toronto. No part of this book may be reproduced or copied in any form without permission from the copyright owner.

www.stepintoreading.com
www.barbie.com

Educators and librarians, for a variety of teaching tools, visit us at
www.randomhouse.com/teachers

Library of Congress Cataloging-in-Publication Data
Jordan, Apple.
Love is in the air / by Apple Jordan ; illustrated by Karen Wolcott. — 1st ed.
      p.    cm. — (Step into reading. Step 1) "Barbie."
ISBN-13: 978-0-375-83517-9 (trade) — ISBN-13: 978-0-375-93517-6 (lib. bdg.)
ISBN-10: 0-375-83517-2 (trade) — ISBN-10: 0-375-93517-7 (lib. bdg.)
I. Wolcott, Karen, ill.   II. Title.   III. Series: Step into reading. Step 1 book.
PZ7.J755Lov   2005    2005002954

Printed in the United States of America  10  9  8  7  6  5  4  3  2  1
First Edition

STEP INTO READING, RANDOM HOUSE, and the Random House colophon are registered trademarks of Random House, Inc.

# Barbie™
# *Love* Is in the *Air*

by Apple Jordan
illustrated by Karen Wolcott

Random House 🏠 New York

# Barbie takes a walk.

# What does she see?

A pair of lovebirds resting in a tree.

A boy with
his teddy bear.

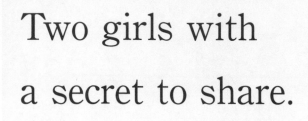

Two girls with
a secret to share.

A picnic lunch
by a creek.

# Kids playing hide-and-seek.

A mother with her baby boy.

A grandpa giving
a brand-new toy.

Roses picked
for someone sweet.

Friends eating

an ice cream treat.

A kiss blown to
Grandma.

# A happy wave hello.

Ducklings and their
mama waddling in a row.

A gallop. A trot.
A piggyback ride.

Barbie sees a box
with a puppy inside!

What a perfect day!

Love is in the air.

When Barbie gets home,

she finds . . .

. . . sweet cookies

waiting there!